Number Skills

When you are using the wipe-clean pen, hold it between your thumb and index finger, resting the pen on your middle finger. Your fingers should be about 1–2 cm away from the pen tip.

Missing numbers

Peppa and George are practising counting from 1 to 5 in Grandpa Pig's vegetable patch. Some numbers have been nibbled away by the birds! Can you fill in the gaps so the numbers read from 1 to 5 in order?

Use the number line at the bottom of the page to help you.

1	2	3	4	5
one	two	three	four	five

Jumbled numbers

Grandpa Pig is tidying up the garden shed. Can you help him by circling the numbers that are in the wrong place?

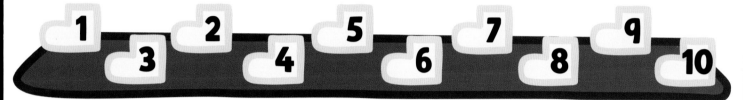

Counting top to bottom

There is one number missing from this tall tower of plant pots. Can you help Peppa work out which one it is? Write the answer in the box.

I need to start counting from the top of the tower, all the way to the bottom.

Adding 1 more

Peppa and Mummy Pig are sorting out old toys for the jumble sale. Can you help them collect the last toy for each pile?

I've found 1 toy car.

Draw 1 more car.

How many cars are there now?

Super effort!

Here are 4 blocks.

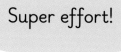

Draw 1 more block.

How many blocks are there now?

At the jumble sale

Look at each group of toys at the jumble sale. Count how many toys there are. If you add 1 more, how many will there be? Finish the number sentences, using the number line below to help you.

add

Now there are ☐ teddies altogether.

add

Now there are ☐ books altogether.

add

Now there are ☐ dolls altogether.

add

Now there are ☐ blocks altogether.

add

Now there are ☐ balls altogether.

6	7	8	9	10
six	seven	eight	nine	ten

How many balls?

Whoops! No one put the balls away after playtime! Help Peppa and Mandy Mouse tidy up by grouping the different kinds of balls together. Draw big circles round all the balls that are the same.

Without counting, write how many balls you can see above in each group.

beach ball	rugby ball	football	tennis ball

How much food?

Look at the shopping baskets below. In each row, circle the basket that has the most food in it.

Can you find the correct answers just by looking, not counting?

Cookie counting

How many cookies are in each jar? Write the numbers in the boxes.

Counting backwards

Zoom! Count backwards down the line of stars to blast off, and then write in the missing numbers.

Start from 10 at the top, and count down. Use the number line to help you.

Nee-naa! Here comes the fire engine. Count backwards from 10 as Miss Rabbit climbs back down the ladder. Write in the missing numbers.

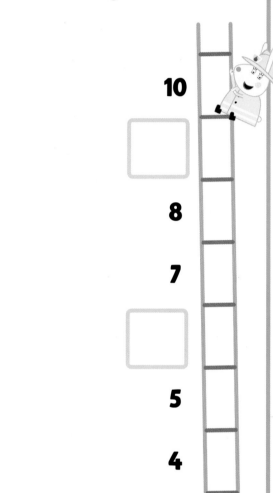

10
9
8
☐

6
5
4
3
☐
1

10
☐
8
7
☐
5
4
3
2
1

10 ten
9 nine
8 eight
7 seven
6 six
5 five
4 four
3 three
2 two
1 one

1 less

Peppa and George are exploring rock pools. Count how many things there are in each rock pool, and then write the answers.
If you take 1 away, how many things will be left?

Use the number line on the opposite page to help you find **1 less** each time.

How many starfish altogether? ☐

1 spins away.

How many are left? ☐

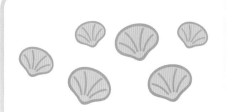

How many shells altogether? ☐

1 washes away.

How many are left? ☐

How many crabs altogether? ☐

1 scuttles away.

How many are left? ☐

Making 5

Let's practise making 5! Count the vehicles in each box, and write in the numbers. What do they add up to each time?

You can make 5 by adding two different numbers together.

I can do it!

There are ☐ diggers.

How many more diggers arrive? ☐

There are ☐ diggers altogether.

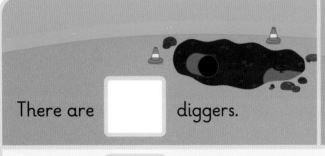

There is ☐ car.

How many more cars drive in? ☐

There are ☐ cars altogether.

There are ☐ planes.

How many more planes land? ☐

There are ☐ planes altogether.

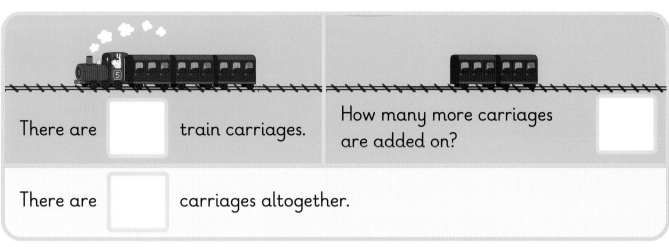

There are ☐ train carriages.

How many more carriages are added on? ☐

There are ☐ carriages altogether.

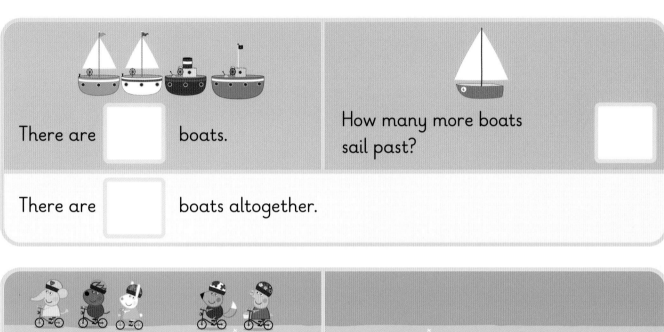

There are ☐ boats.

How many more boats sail past? ☐

There are ☐ boats altogether.

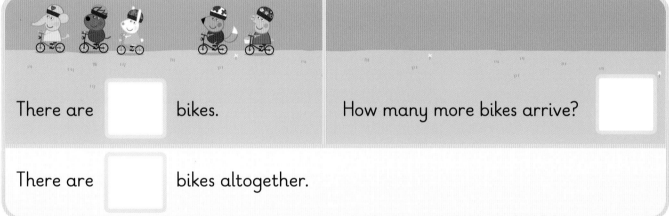

There are ☐ bikes.

How many more bikes arrive? ☐

There are ☐ bikes altogether.

How to make 5

Draw lines to match the pairs of numbers that make 5 altogether.

0	2
1	5
2	0
3	3
4	1
5	4

Making 10

Peppa and her friends are learning which pairs of numbers make 10.
Use your number skills to help them.

Circle 2 flowers in this planter. How many are left?

2 and ☐ make 10 altogether.

I'm going to count the flowers that are not in the circle!

Circle 4 sweets in this jar. How many are left?

4 and ☐ make 10 altogether.

Circle 5 crayons on this tray. How many are left?

5 and ☐ make 10 altogether.

Circle 1 cupcake on the plate. How many are left? ☐

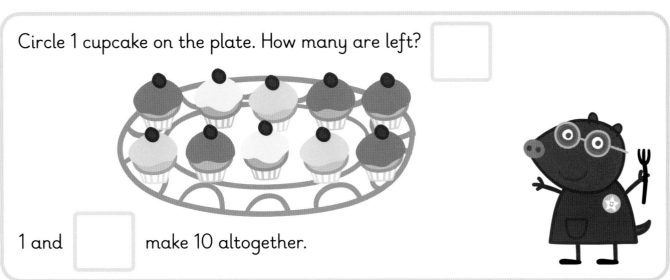

1 and ☐ make 10 altogether.

Circle 3 blocks. How many are left? ☐

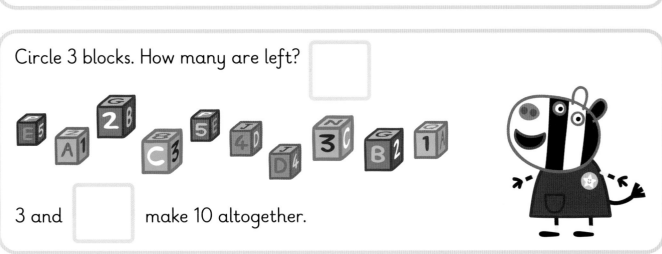

3 and ☐ make 10 altogether.

Other ways of making 10

Complete these number sentences. What do you notice about them?

6 and ☐ equal 10.   9 and ☐ equal 10.

7 and ☐ equal 10.   10 and ☐ equal 10.

8 and ☐ equal 10.   0 and ☐ equal 10.

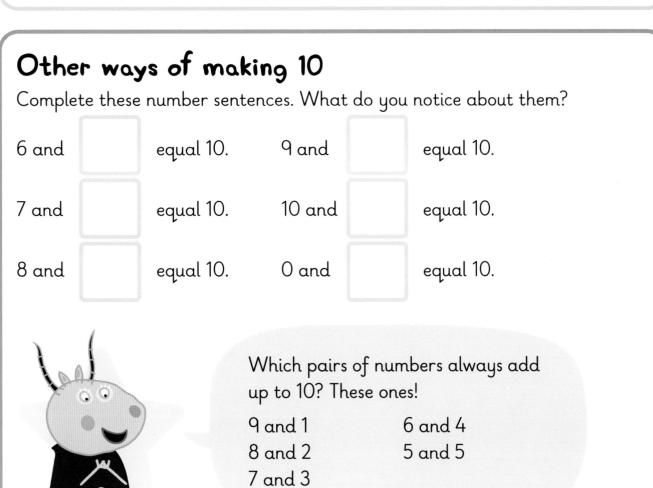

Which pairs of numbers always add
up to 10? These ones!

9 and 1   6 and 4
8 and 2   5 and 5
7 and 3

Lots of spots!

George has found some ladybirds in the garden. They all have a different number of spots. Can you help to double them?

Doubling means adding together two numbers that are the same.

Like us! 1 panda and 1 panda make 2 pandas altogether!

Count the spots on each ladybird's wing. Then, draw the same number of spots on the opposite wing. Add the spots together to double the number you first saw.

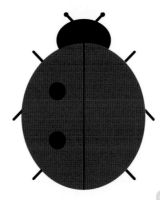

Double 2 is ☐ .

Double 3 is ☐ .

Double 4 is ☐ .

Double 5 is ☐ .

Busy bees halving

Buzz! The bees are going back to their hives. Count the bees in each picture. Draw one circle round half of them and another circle round the other half. Make sure there is the same number of bees in each circle!

Halving is sharing something equally between two.

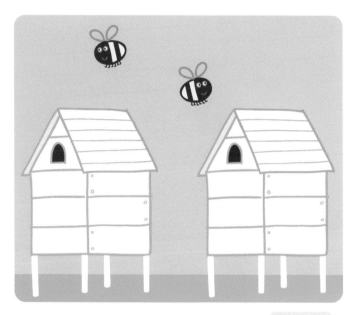

Half of 2 is ▢ .

Half of 8 is ▢ .

Half of 6 is ▢ .

Half of 4 is ▢ .

P, actice makes pe, fe t!

Let's use your number skills to find the correct answers to these questions!

Which number is missing from the flag? Write it in.

1   2   3   5

Without counting them, write how many crayons you can see.

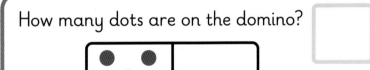

Count the socks. How many are there?

Draw 1 more. How many are there now?

How many dots are on the domino?

Draw the same number of dots on the other side. How many dots are there altogether?

I love number games!

Everyone loves number games!

16